For Owen
—D.W.L.

Visit us on the Web! www.randomhouse.com/kids

Educators and librarians, for a variety of teaching tools,
visit us at www.randomhouse.com/teachers

Library of Congress Cataloging-in-Publication Data
Landolf, Diane Wright.
What a good big brother! / by Diane Wright Landolf ;
illustrated by Steve Johnson and Lou Fancher. — 1st ed.
p. cm.
Summary: Cameron is always ready to help when his baby sister cries, whether
by handing wipes to his father during a diaper change or finding the nursing pillow
for his mother, until one day, when no one else can stop Sadie's tears, her big
brother succeeds and gets a wonderful reward.
ISBN 978-0-375-84258-0 (trade) — ISBN 978-0-375-94258-7 (lib. bdg.)
[1. Brothers and sisters—Fiction. 2. Babies—Fiction. 3. Family life—Fiction.]
I. Johnson, Steve, ill. II. Fancher, Lou, ill. III. Title.
PZ7.L2317345Wha 2008
[E]—dc22
2006015181

Book design by Lou Fancher

MANUFACTURED IN CHINA  10 9 8 7 6 5 4 3 2 1  First Edition

For Dave, Joel, and Tyler
—S.J. & L.F.

# What a Good Big Brother!

By **Diane Wright Landolf** • Paintings by **Steve Johnson** & **Lou Fancher**

Random House 🏠 New York

Cameron loved his new baby sister, Sadie. He loved to pat her head, and rub her tummy, and kiss her sweet little toes.

"Why is Sadie crying?" Cameron asked.

"She needs a diaper change," his dad said. "Do you want to help?"

"Yes," said Cameron.

Waaaaaaaaaaaaaaaaaa

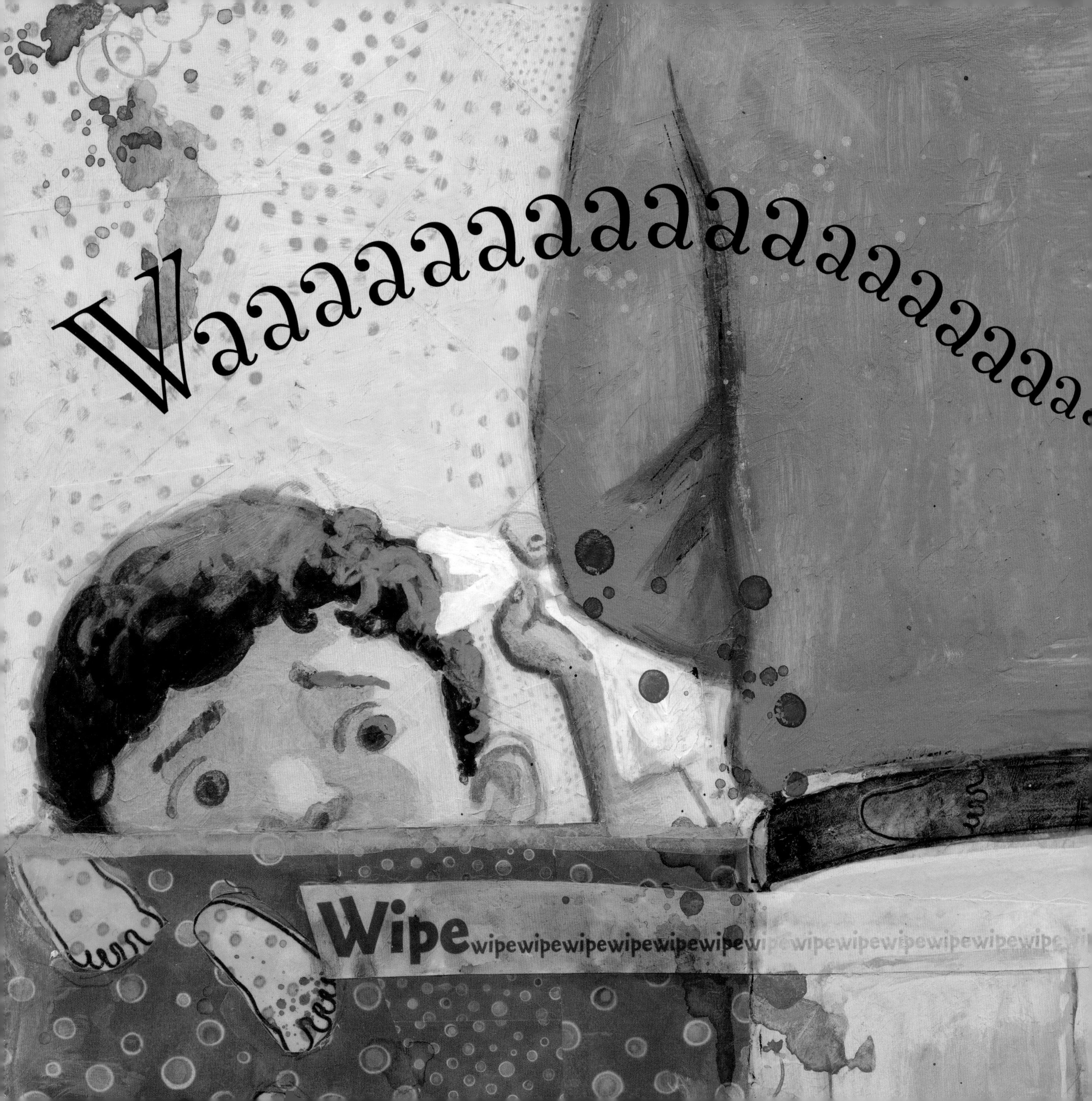

aaaaaaaaaaaaaaaaaaaaaaaaaaaaaaaaaaaa

He followed his dad and Sadie into the nursery. Sadie was crying the whole way. His dad put Sadie down on the changing table. He unsnapped her sleeper. Cameron handed him a wipe. Sadie cried.

Cameron's dad took off Sadie's diaper. "Yowza!" he said. Cameron handed him five more wipes in a hurry.

Once Sadie had on a clean, dry diaper and a clean, dry sleeper, she quieted down. "Sadie, my baby, the pretty little lady," Cameron's dad sang. He smiled at her as he snapped her back up. Cameron patted her head.

"What a good big brother," said his dad.

patpatpat

"Why is Sadie crying?" Cameron asked.

"She's tired," his mom whispered. "Do you want to help us put her down for a nap?"

"Yes," said Cameron. He followed his mom and dad and Sadie into his parents' room. Sadie was crying the whole way.

Cameron's mom put Sadie down in her bassinet. Cameron climbed up on the bed to look at her. Sadie cried. Cameron's mom started singing a lullaby. Cameron's dad rocked the bassinet. Cameron reached down and rubbed Sadie's tummy until she closed her eyes.

Then nobody said a word.

Waaaaaaaaaaaaaa

aaaaaaaaaaaaaaaaaaaaaaaaaaaaaaaaaaa

"Why is Sadie crying?" Cameron asked.

"She's hungry," his mom said. "Do you know where her nursing pillow is?"

"Yes," said Cameron. He ran into his bedroom and picked up the pillow from the floor, where Sadie had been lying earlier while he showed her his trucks. Then he ran back to the living room and handed the pillow to his mom. Sadie was crying the whole time.

Cameron's mom tucked the nursing pillow around herself. Cameron climbed up on the couch next to her. Sadie cried.

Then suddenly, Sadie was quiet. She was busy eating. Cameron kissed Sadie's sweet little toes.

"What a good big brother," said his mom.

"Why is Sadie crying?" Cameron asked.

"I don't know," said his dad.

"Is she hungry?" Cameron asked.

"I just fed her," said his mom.

"And I just changed her," said his dad.

"We've picked her up," said his mom.

"We've put her down," said his dad.

"We've walked her, we've rocked her, we've sung to her," Cameron's mom said.

"Sometimes babies just cry," said his dad.

Waaaaaaaaaaaaaaa.

Cameron sat down on the floor next to his baby sister. "Poor Sadie. Poor little lady," he said. Sadie cried.

Cameron reached out to pat her head. Gently, gently, he patted her. Sadie's crying slowly quieted down to a whimper. Cameron's parents sat up straight.

waaa

aaaaaaa

Cameron rubbed Sadie's tummy. She stopped whimpering and stared at him. Cameron's parents stared, too.

Now Cameron kissed Sadie's sweet little toes. He kissed one foot, then the other. And then something happened that had never happened before.

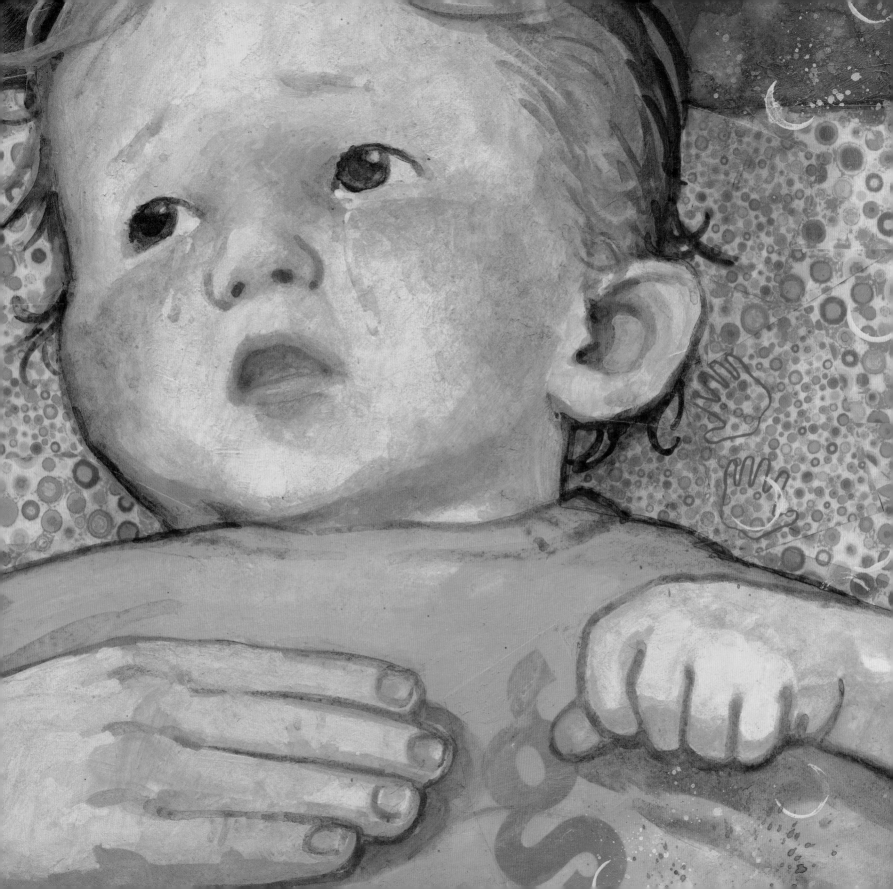

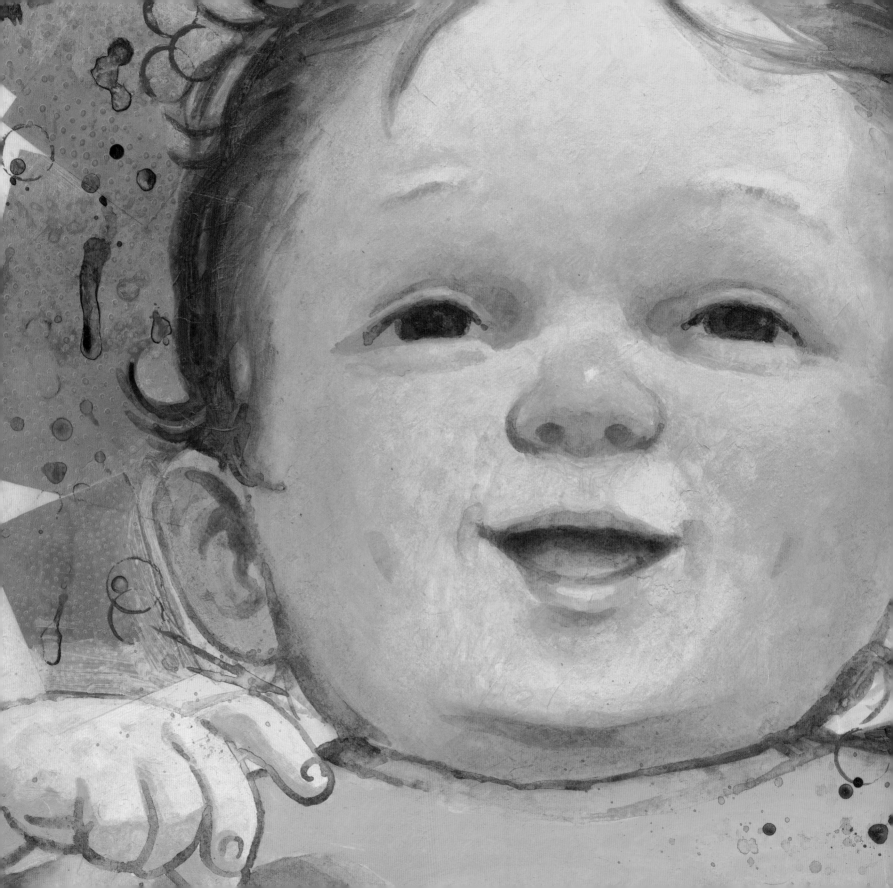

Sadie smiled.

"She's smiling!" said Cameron.

"She's smiling!" said his parents.

"What a smile!" said his mom.

"What a grin!" said his dad.

"And what a good big brother!"